DATE

This book belongs to

_____

whose superpower is

_____

Creative Director: Tricia Legault • Art Director: Nelson Greenfield
Editorial Director: Guy Davis

Printed at ColorDynamics, Allen, Texas 75002

1 2 3 4 5 6 7 8 9 10   01 00

ISBN 1-57064-950-2

Library of Congress Number 00-100702

PAJAMA SAM™

Mission to the Moon

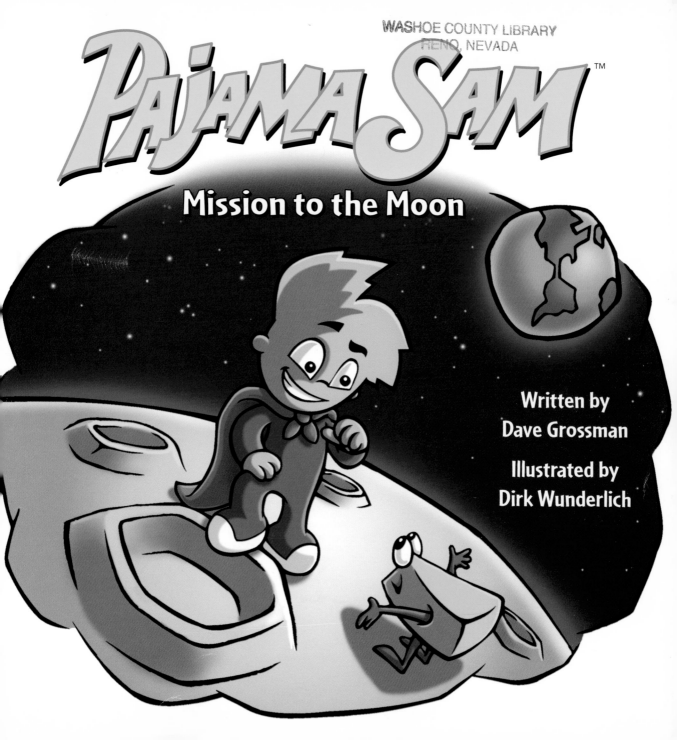

Written by
Dave Grossman

Illustrated by
Dirk Wunderlich

Pajama Sam is the world's youngest superhero! Like his idol, Pajama Man, he helps those in need and battles evil and injustice.

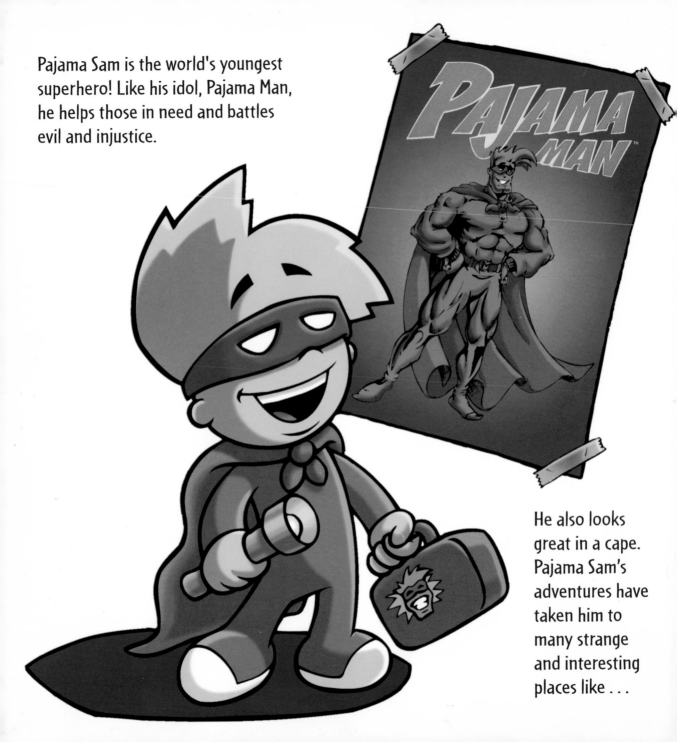

He also looks great in a cape. Pajama Sam's adventures have taken him to many strange and interesting places like . . .

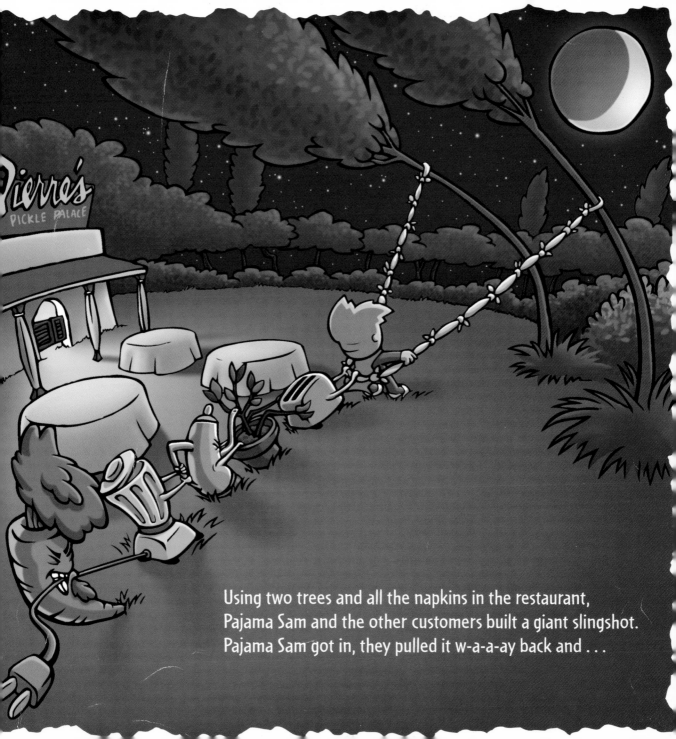

Using two trees and all the napkins in the restaurant,
Pajama Sam and the other customers built a giant slingshot.
Pajama Sam got in, they pulled it w-a-a-ay back and . . .

After Pajama Sam recovered from his loony lunar launch, he set out to find the moon's light switch.

Let's see, dust ...

craters ...

more dust ...

Pushing and pulling with all his might,
Pajama Sam turned the moon to full.

In desperation, Pajama Sam
tried to jump back to Earth.

Jack showed Pajama Sam around the moon.
Moon City was huge, and it was all underground.